To my Auntie Erna and Erika, thank you for your unending support and love.
I hope I've made you proud.

To my nieces and nephews, I love you and remember, Mommy knows best!

Love,

Stacey

MANDY

Tangled In A Web

Story by: **Stacey Gardin**

Illustrated by: **Stephanie**

Mandy was sad.
She wanted a pet,

So she went to her mom,
But her Mom said
"Not yet".

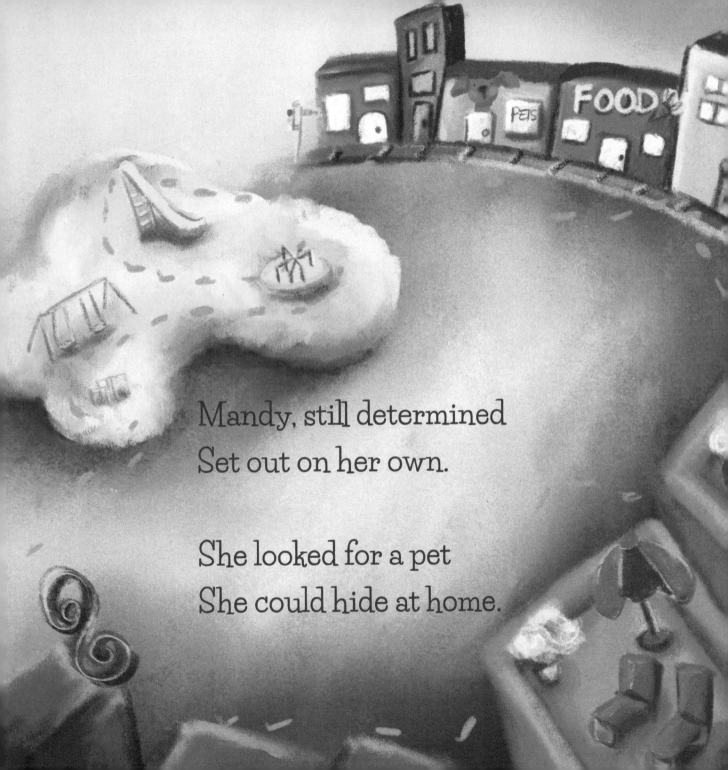

Mandy, still determined
Set out on her own.

She looked for a pet
She could hide at home.

"Maybe an elephant, we both love nuts!

He sure could help if I'm stuck in a rut"

"But when mom comes home, where on earth could he hide?

There's gonna be trouble with his big back side"

She ate a few nuts
and let out a laugh

She shrieked
"I've got it!
I'll get a giraffe!"

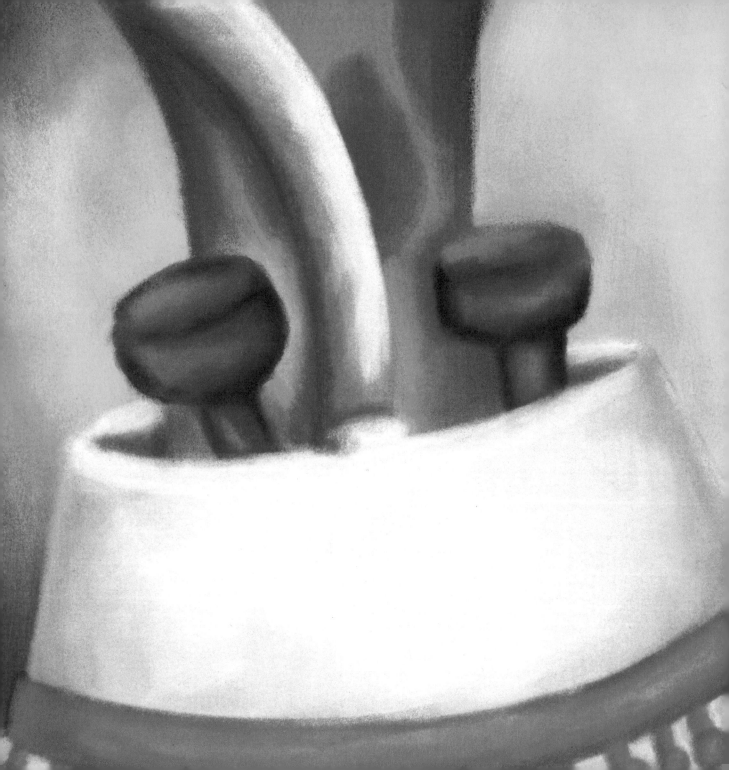

"I could ride her all day and look at her spots.

I could even draw lines and connect the dots!"

"But where would she hide when the sun begins to fade?

Mom's sure to see her underneath her lamp shade."

Running out of ideas,
she sat in her wagon.

Her eyes lit up,
"I know! A dragon!"

"We could stay up late, and he could roast smores.

Mom wouldn't know, we'd wait til she snores!"

"But when she wakes up, she'd let out a wail!

There's no way I could hide his long tail!"

"A unicorn, yes!
That's surely a winner!"

"She could save me from peas.
Yuck! They're so tragic!

She'd make them disappear,
by using her magic!"

"But where will she go, so mother won't know?

She's sure hard to stow, the way that she glows!"

Dogs were too furry.

Cats were too...

Then she thought,

"Crickets!
Yes, crickets
will do!"

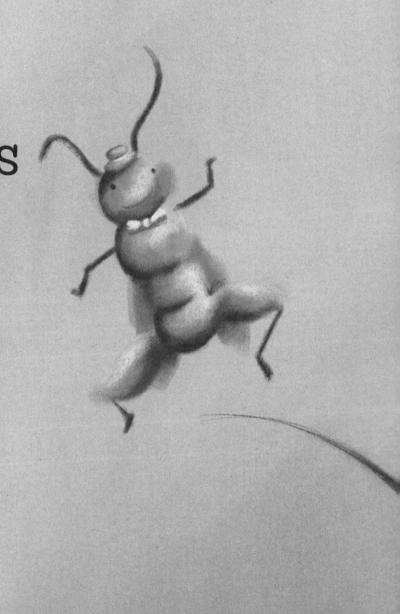

But one by one

They just hopped
away.

Then creepy, crawling spiders
Came out to play.

Mandy hated spiders. She
yelled, "Mom, Mom
help!"

"Make them go away!"
She said as she yelped.

Her mom then asked,
"What brought them
inside?"

"I don't know; I don't know"
She said as she cried.

A few days passed
 No bugs in sight.

Then a big hairy spider
Crawled right up to her thigh!

Mandy was shaking and
Utterly spooked.

She broke down and told
her mother the truth.

She said, "I'm so sorry,
So sorry I lied..."

Her mom held her and
whispered,
"I knew the whole time."

They got rid of the spider
And cleaned up the mess.

Mandy felt lighter
With that weight off her chest.

Her mother was glad
That she finally confessed.

Mandy proudly proclaimed, "Mothers know best!"

Mandy was patient
Obedient too

And before she knew it,
She had a pet too!

The End

STACEY GARDIN

Stacey Gardin is an American-Trinidadian author. Born in a desert out west, splashed onto a Caribbean island, and landing in the south, Stacey has been exposed to many different cultures. Throughout them all, she learned that kids have similar desires and ways of trying to achieve them (although not always well thought out). Her first book, Mandy: Tangled in a Web, explores the journey of a little girl wanting her first pet. Stacey takes the reader through an exciting journey of finding the right fit for Mandy. All of her lies spin a web of chaos that she doesn't know how to escape on her own.

www.staceygardin.com